Blood in the Darkness

Sir Patrick Bijou

Helping others without expectation of anything in return has been proven to lead to increased happiness and satisfaction in life.

I would love to give you the chance to experience that same feeling during your reading or listening experience today...

All it takes is a few moments of your time to answer one simple question:

Would you make a difference in the life of someone you've never met—without spending any money or seeking recognition for your good will?

If so, I have a small request for you.

If you've found value in your reading or listening experience today, I humbly ask that you take a brief moment right now to leave an honest review of this book. It won't cost you anything but 30 seconds of your time—just a few seconds to share your thoughts with others.

Your voice can go a long way in helping someone else find the same inspiration and knowledge that you have.

Are you familiar with leaving a review for an Audible, Kindle, or e-reader book? If so, it's simple:

If you're on Audible: just hit the three dots in the top right of your device, click rate & review, then leave a few sentences about the book along with your star rating.

If you're reading on Kindle or an e-reader, simply scroll to the last page of the book and swipe up—the review should prompt from there.

If you're on a Paperback or any other physical format of this book, you can find the book page on Amazon (or wherever you bought this) and leave your review right there.

PRELUDE

What if immortality was a curse instead of a gift?

In *Blood in the Darkness*, Stefan, once a humble painter from the 14th century, finds himself trapped in a never-ending life of loneliness and thirst—thirst for blood, food, and forbidden desires. Centuries ago, Stefan was wrongfully accused of being evil and was burned alive. But death wasn't the end. Now, he wanders through the shadows of modern society, cursed with a vampire's immortality.

While Stefan tries to keep a low profile, he can't escape the haunting emptiness of his existence. But when a stormy night brings Natasha into his world, Stefan's control starts to slip. The attraction between them is instant, but so is the danger. Stefan's desire is darker than most, and his past is filled with terrifying secrets.

As women in the city disappear without a trace, bodies occasionally surface, each with mysterious bite marks. The police are baffled, and rumours of vampires are dismissed as fantasy. But Stefan knows better. He hides from the daylight, stalks the night, and struggles to balance the line between predator and protector.

Will Natasha be Stefan's salvation—or his next victim?

Blood in the Darkness weaves a tale of erotic tension, dark passions, and the torment of eternal life. Are you ready to explore the dark side of desire?

Grab your copy of *Blood in the Darkness* today!

ABOUT THE AUTHOR

Sir Patrick Bijou lives and writes from the United Kingdom and is the author of several books on finance and fiction. He is known for his extraordinary skills in settling and negotiating peace settlements and international law and is a prodigious legal and political adviser. His diverse writing ability has been influenced by many experiences, making him the success he is today.

Sir Patrick has written books and articles about the liberation of people, highlighting the issues of those whom the literary world of creative writing has not enlightened. His expedition into content writing has made him a remarkably inspired author and professional communicator.

He has written over 45 non-fictional and fictional books spanning different genres.

Finding his Books.

To find out more about Sir Patrick, visit his website.

www.sirpatrickbijou.com
www.bijouebook.com

What is immortality, and is it a curse or a gift? A physical body can never be immortal and dies too easily. However, the soul is immortal. Immortality can be a curse at times as well as a gift, depending on the situation. The curse being the boredom of living so long. It can get very boring as there is so much that can really be done to stay entertained. One more negative aspect is to endure the pain when the body gets destroyed either by being involved in an accident or attempting to get rid of vampires.

Stefan is such an individual who once used to be a painter in the 14th Century. He loved to paint portraits of young ladies. He never harmed any woman, nor did he ever have any bad intentions for any of the girls he painted, the society still believed him to be an evil man. He accidentally spilled paint on one of his clients one day. She complained to the crowd nearby. This gave them sufficient reasoning to punish the evil and burnt him alive despite his repeated apologies.

Following the event, a few days later, the entire village was empty. Half of the villages had died while others fled. Rumor has it that Stefan turned into some demon and sought revenge, while others say that this was an act of God.

Stefan has no recollection of the events as centuries passed. He neither knows why he has to carry the burden of living a never-ending life. All he has now is a lonely life and a thirst for blood, delicious food, and sex.

* * *

There have been reports of young sexy women disappearing or showing up dead randomly. The police have been searching for any connections; however, the bodies would turn up once in a couple of months or even in a few years. The case keeps being closed and re-opened. The only connection between all the murders has been bite marks all over the women's bodies.

There were no fingerprint marks anywhere that could help the police trace the killer and no strange news of weird pregnancies or monsters walking the streets. The news channels too never pay too much attention to these minute details. The loved ones' families lost claim of demonic or vampiric activities; however, all those thoughts are shrugged off. Not many people believe in this in modern times.

* * *

Stefan found an old abandoned house and preferred to spend the day sleeping indoors as direct sunlight seemed to damage his skin. He mostly preferred to wander about late at night.

He worked nights at a nearby McDonald's to earn enough money to buy clothes or eat out at restaurants. He would usually get free food at work. Eating the food kept his desire for blood under control. He needed to ensure that he kept a low profile.

He liked the night shift as it was rare for a hot girl to show up, mostly due to the location, however, also the time of his shift. The McDonald was located far off the highway next to a truck repair shop. He mostly had mechanics and truck drivers showing up. He worked parttime from 10 pm to 5 am.

There were times when girls did show up either alone or with friends. It was difficult for Stefan to control his lust. It was almost the end of his shift on a Friday morning. He was looking forward to the weekend. It's been a while since his last feast, almost a couple of years.

Minutes before his shift ended, a woman stepped into the restaurant. She was drenched in water with all her clothes sticking to her body. It had been pouring all night. She must have been caught in the rain somehow. She was wearing a tank top with a deep cut neck. It was a white tank top that was now wet, revealing the lady's beautiful round breasts and nipples. She was a real beauty with blonde hair.

"Do you have any towels or any change of clothes by any chance? My car broke down not too far from here, but I got caught in the rain," she asked. Stefan could not get his eyes off her; however, he was experienced being in such situations many times. He calmly responded that he does not have any here, but if she didn't mind, his house is not too far, and she can wait for her car to be fixed there while she dried herself.

Natasha didn't see any better alternatives given the situation and agreed to go to Stefan's house.

Stefan asked his co-worker who took over the shift to ask the nearby mechanics to pick up her car from the described location and call Stefan's cell once done.

Natasha followed Stefan to his car. He drove an old beater Honda Civic. "Sorry, I'm getting your car seat all wet." Natasha was feeling quite embarrassed about the situation. However, she didn't understand why, but she felt relaxed around Stefan. She felt a little excitement or happiness within her now that she was alone with him.

"Don't worry about the seat. The car is ancient anyway. I hope you don't get sick. you have been wet for quite a while." Stefan drove home. Natasha felt it was weird of him living in such a secluded area with no one around. His house was even more dilapidated than his car. She should be scared of entering a house with a stranger, yet she felt relaxed and at home.

Stefan handed her a towel and showed her the washroom. He instructed her that the bathroom will have bathrobes that she can wear while her clothes dried. "Oh, thank you so much; I don't know how I can repay your favor."

"Don't worry. We have plenty of time for that. I forgot to mention, the Mechanics found your car, and it seems like some of the parts got filled with water, and it will take a week for it to be repaired." Stefan lied on the duration. It was only to take 2 hours to fix the car, yet, he did not want to miss the opportunity to spend a week with such a hottie.

Natasha was puzzled about what will she do for a week. She can not live with a stranger for that long. "You can stay here for the week, I don't mind," added Stefan. Natasha surprisingly nodded in agreement.

Nathasha took a nice hot shower, dried herself, and found the bathrobes in one of the closets. The robes were really nice and clean and perfectly fitting. The white robes covered most of her body, showing a small amount of cleavage.

The duo ordered some pizza for breakfast. "What is your name? I forgot to ask." Natasha asked while sitting at the dining table.

"That's alright, and it's been an eventful morning. I am Stefan, and yours?"

"Natasha. How long have you been living here."

"I have lived here since as far as I can remember. It is quite abandoned though it is where I feel at home." Stefan replied. "You should get some sleep; you must be tired," he added.

Stefan continued to admire her hot 27-year-old body. He also ensured to make as much eye contact with her to ensure he could control her mind. Each time he made contact with her, the passion burnt stronger within Natasha. She was not sure, but with every single passing moment, she felt a greater desire to throw herself into his arms.

After finishing up breakfast, Stefan showed Natasha the room she could use. It was in the basement with absolutely no windows or light source. There was just an old school oil lamp that barely lit up the surrounding of where she stood.

"I will be in the next room. Let me know if you need anything," Stefan instructed.

"Do you have to be in another room? I mean, we both can share this room or yours," replied Natasha. She was partly surprised that she just said that.

Being in a dark room was turning her on even more. She could not resist it anymore.

Stefan walked closer to her. As he approached Natasha, her breathing intensified. She gasped as he took her into his arms and brought her even closer towards him. His body felt as cold as ice. She could feel his hardness between her legs. He started to grind his member against her as his lips touched her lips.

Careful not to bite so soon, Stefan started to kiss Natasha more passionately. She let out a soft moan after each kiss. Slowly he moved down her cheeks, her neck, and her breasts. He sucked on her nipples, softly kneading the other.

He pulled off her robes with a sudden force and took off his own clothes, and pushed her onto the bed. Natasha observed the build of her lover; he was really built with a muscular body.

She was amazed at the sight of the 7-inch member. She had several boyfriends in the past, but none of them could beat this passion.

She spread her arms forward, inviting Stefan into her arms. He climbed the bed and slowly crawled on top of her. She pulled him into her arms and started to smooch.

The warmth of her body was relaxing the tension built into Stefan over the past several years. He could get used to being in such warmth all the time. The aroma of her young blood was irresistible. As he kissed her soft lips, he could not stop himself from taking a few sips of her youth.

Natasha's eyes widened, and she let out a muffled scream as his fangs dipped deep into her lips, but the pain soon disappeared, replaced by incredible pleasure. Stefan relished the softness of her lips and the warm tastiness of her blood, careful not to drink too much.

He lifted his head and looked into her eyes. "My baby, you have the sweetest blood I have ever tasted."

"Take me, my love; I am yours. Take whatever you desire." Natasha replied. She gasped as Stefan pushed his hard cock deep into her excited pussy. Natasha moaned as he repeatedly pumped his member in and out of her, going a bit deeper each time.

He grabbed her tits and started to squeeze them as he fucked her. Natasha's body trembled, and her eyes rolled over as he hit her orgasm. It was getting easier for Stefan to go deeper as his dick was lubricated with the girl's hot juices.

"Too deep, my love, you are in too deep... it's too much," moaned Natasha as she hit another orgasm. Shortly after, Stefan too climaxed as she felt his hot wad gushing deep into her womb.

Stefan dropped down to her neck for another bite. The sudden attack pushed Natasha over the edge again as her lover fed on her.

* * *

Hours later, Natasha woke up with an aching body and a lot of weakness. The room was now pitch dark as the oil lamp had run out of oil.

She was alone in the room naked. The mind control of Stefan was broken; she vaguely remembered being drenched and meeting a stranger. This was probably his house. She neither remembered how he looked, nor did she remember his name.

She managed to find her way to the basement stairs and made her way to the main house lobby. The stairs creaked at each step. It felt that they might break any instance. She could not find any clothes and was wandering the house naked.

She found her clothes in the washroom. She changed quickly and rushed outside. She found her car parked outside and found it weird. She never paid for the repairs.

She sat in her car and returned home back to her daily routines.

* * *

Stefan ensured not to drink all her blood or end her life. He really hated the idea of the possibility of having wives or girls showing up dead. One night stands were the best as there was no way anyone could trace activities back to him.

*

It has been a few months since Natasha's encounter with Stefan. All the bite wounds have healed, and she no longer has any weakness. She could no longer focus on anything anymore. She had never craved sex before so much that it interfered with work. It seems like she was longing for a long-lost lover yet, she doesn't remember much about him.

Natasha was one of the girls who prioritized her work and carrier as the first choice. Everything else came after. Since she visited the old house, things have changed. Sex seemed to be the only priority now. To relax her feelings, she tried meditation, then masturbation, and even dating. Things were getting worse, and sex therapists were of no help either.

Stefan had let her leave on purpose. He did not want to drink all her blood or make her a slave. Vampires have feelings like humans, and as they age, the sensations intensify. The only difference is vampires have a stronger will to control the emotions, almost shutting them off. He lived a neutral life and had no feelings of love, longing, happiness, or sorrow. If he had not controlled them, an immortal life could lead to an immortal depression.

His impact on Natasha had left permanent effects on her as well as himself. Stefan had managed to move on, but Natasha still needed him.

Natasha decided that she will look for her answers back in the same home. Taking a few weeks off from work on health grounds and started on her journey.

She had saved the home address in her GPS. It was about a 30 minutes drive. She was able to remember how the house looked and knew she was at the right address.

She opened the door carefully, making sure that it doesn't come off its hinges. The house was completely dark. There was no way sunlight could make it through. Each window had been sealed with several layers of wooden planks. The floor tiles were all damaged.

Her only light source being her mobile torch, she barely could see where she was going. Judging how things looked, it doesn't seem like anyone has made an effort to refurnish or renovate this house.

There was no one on the main floor, but she heard moaning from the basement as she approached the stairs. It sounded like a girl's voice.

"Ahh...yes...baby...harder..harder... ahhh.harder!"

A blonde girl was in bed with Stefan.

She should be feeling hurt or at least jealous about the fact that she was not in his arms right now. Strangely she was getting excited by witnessing the scene.

She couldn't stop watching. Natasha didn't realize when her hand moved to her pussy and when she had started fingering herself, almost moaning as loudly as the blonde.

Stefan finally climaxed, releasing his juice within her and drinking a few sips of her red life from her lips. He got up and cleaned up the blood and sweat from his body. He noticed Natasha in the room. Natasha, too, had climaxed. She straightened her dress as the Dracula approached her. She wanted more, but first, she had more pressing questions.

Natasha sat on one of the couches in the bedroom wearing a concise v-neck puff sleeve mini dress that tightly wrapped her body, defining her bosoms and butts well. The deep neck showed a deep cleavage while pushed her big boobs up, making them look even more prominent and rounder. She intended to seduce Stefan. The aroma of her blood and her hot young body was driving the lust within Stefan to its limits.

"You came back?" Stefan asked Natasha.

"Is she dead? Were you drinking her blood?" asked Natasha ignoring Stefan's question. She was more curious than was she scared or surprised.

"She is alive, just tired, and I was drinking her blood," Stefan responded with a calm voice.

"Did you drink mine as well?" Natasha inquired immediately.

Stefan responded with a nod.

"Will I turn into a vampire?"

"No, just drinking your blood is not enough. A ritual needs to be performed for that to happen. It is still not a guarantee that you will turn into a vampire."

"But movies show that girls become vampires in one bite?" Natasha clarified, sounding a little disappointed.

Stefan laughed at her innocence. "Horror movie directors make movies after reading superstitious blogs on the internet. It is all fake. The close only part is that you can kill some of the lower-ranked vampires by stabbing, chopping off the head, or by fire."

"Lower ranked vampires?"

"Yes, If an immortal vampire desires to have slaves, he or she can perform the ritual. If the ritual is successful, then the human they chose becomes their slave. The slave will not be immortal and can die easily."

"So you are an immortal. How do you become one? So No one can kill you?" Natasha now even more curious.

"Immortality is something that you get as a gift. It's rare. You cannot obtain it by following any steps or drinking out of a fountain. It is the will of a power beyond any human or vampiric control. If anyone were to destroy me, my soul would still exist, and slowly I will get my body back. It is a slow and painful process, but technically I cannot be wiped out permanently." Stefan answered.

Stefan read her mind to get answers to his questions.

Would you like something to eat? Stefan asked Natasha.

They ate some leftover chicken. Natasha helped clean up, and they went upstairs, which too was dark.

"Why is the whole house dark. I thought you couldn't die?" Natasha wondered.

"I can't, but the UV rays hurt my eyes and skin. It is more of an annoyance to get damaged skin and re-heal."

Natasha suddenly stopped mid-flight and kissed Stefan on his lips. Her chest was heaving as her breathing quickened.

The sudden kiss took Stefan by surprise too.

Natasha was excited as she spread out her arms, inviting her lover. Her mind and body were totally under Stefan's control. He ensured to keep it that way to avoid interruptions.

He walked towards Natasha, slowly teasing her by taking his time. He slowly kissed her navel over her dress through to her breasts. He sucked her protruding nipples over her dress, at time burying his face between her tits.

The warmth of her body was giving life to his phallus. She could feel his member grow and push against her snatch. She moaned as his dick pushed her wet clitoris through her panties and was driving her crazy with excitement.

Suddenly Stefan buried his fangs into her neck and slowly sipped the oozing warm blood. He was carefully licking the stream that trickled past his lips.

He slowly kneaded her tits and rubbed his dick along her pussy. Natasha's entire body quivered as the excitement reached its peak. She let out a small whine as her body climaxed.

Stefan moved towards her legs and slowly undid her undies. He was kissing her thighs slowly and carefully, moving closer to her hole. Natasha arched her back and screamed into climax again as his fangs buried deep into her privates, sipping on her tender juices. He was still massaging her breasts to keep the blood flowing. She grabbed the back of his head with both hands and pushed his face closer to her pussy.

He ensured to sip till the blood trickled through his bite wounds. Natasha's body trembled with the massive amounts of pleasures hitting her. Stefan further buried his face in her tits, kissing, biting, and sucking. He kept at it for a while.

"Please, baby, fuck me now... I want you in me," Natasha begged him to fuck her.

With one more rip, Stefan completely ripped the dress. Stefan lifted Natasha, rested her back against the wall, and thrust his member into her aching pussy. She wrapped her legs around him and grabbed onto his shoulders. Natasha loved the pleasure of his member pushing deep into her and the searing pain left by his bite.

She pulled his face down to her breasts and offered her nipples as he fucked her. Stefan sucked her erect nipples, carefully pressing the necessary points to get her milk to start flowing.

He slowly drank the cocktail of her blood and milk as the couple made love for the next few hours.

Stefan could not resist and returned to her neck and kept drinking her blood hungrily. His cock was still inside her. He pumped his dick hard and climaxed. Natasha whimpered in pain and pleasure as she fainted.

Stefan loved the attention he was getting. He finished up with Natasha and headed downstairs. Both beauties had been fucked their brains out and will wake up in the next few days as their bodies rebuild the amount of blood Stefan had sipped during sex.

He preferred to drink from their boobs since the amount of blood lost was minimum and posed no risk to their life. Drinking from the neck too much could prove dangerous.

He didn't tell Natasha that the movies show that Vampires drink all the girls' blood in a few bites. That was not true. It takes hours for a vampire to drink a girl dry in one sitting, and that too if the vampire was only surviving on blood.

It's rare for vampires to feed only on blood, though. It would be like eating the same recipe for the rest of your life.

***

Stefan decided to leave his job and house and move to a new area. He took Natasha and Samantha on the trip along with him. They moved out of the cities and back into the country area with a lesser population.

Stefan hired a driver to drive his car while Stefan had fun with his ladies in the back seat.

There were beautiful landscapes to visit, hot women, and on the plus side, Law enforcement was on the lower side; The police force's size being a maximum of 3 members. He did not intend to go on a killing spree, but there was always a risk of getting caught. The closest police backup was three hours giving Stefan enough time to escape.

***

Almost every city or town always has a haunted house that people tend to avoid. The Priestley House, a historic Mississippi mansion, one of the nation's spookiest Haunted Houses for sale, was the perfect spot to move into.

Stefan's neighbor was a hot woman in her early thirties. She lived alone as her husband was always traveling for work and returned home once every few months, sometimes a few years. She had a few friends that would meet her once in a while. Nancy's friends were too busy hooking up with young guys in town. They only visited her if they broke up with their boyfriend or needed help with something. Nancy was now used to staying alone. She had found ways to keep herself occupied and preferred it this way.

Nancy noticed someone moved into the haunted house across the street. Initially, she thought she saw ghosts, but she saw Stefan eat and watch TV, sometimes even have sex with Natasha and Samantha. His activities didn't seem paranormal.

She felt a desire building up within her as she saw Stefan passionately make out with Natasha. It's been a while since she had sex, and was craving a massive dick in her. She was surprised with her urge for sex as she never felt so slutty before. She had always been a well-cultured girl staying within her limits. She ignored the feelings and calmed herself down. She should be loyal to her husband.

Stefan had noticed Nancy as well. They would smile back at each other whenever they saw each other. Stefan was slowly trying to control her mind, but Nancy seemed to have to sway her feelings.

Stefan had invited her for dinner on several occasions, only to face disappointment. Nancy made an excuse each time. It was not the right thing to go to a man's house alone at night, especially when her husband is not with her.

Nancy's refusal was making Stefan impatient. He could smell the aroma of her warm blood all the way from her house. He could not control it anymore.

Stefan could travel short distances and enter through tight spots by transforming into a cloud of mist. This ability was ineffective for multiple entries or long distances. It demanded high stamina.

After a tiring day, Nancy finished up her routine and got ready for bed. She wore her see-through lacy nightgown displaying her pink pussy lips and nipples. It kept her cool and comfortable at night.

Stefan waited for her to sleep, entered through her bedroom windows, and slowly changed back to his standard form.

Nancy was sleeping calmly in her bed. Stefan accidentally dropped the photo frame of her husband and her waking up.

"Who are you? What are you doing in my bedroom? Nancy asked, covering herself in a blanket.

She inched backward as Stefan approached her. He ensured that she has a constant gaze in his eyes.

"Speak up. What do you want? Asked Nancy this time, she didn't have the same authority in her voice this time. There was something about his eyes that was distracting her.

"Look in my eyes, Nancy. I have so much love for you. Why have you been ignoring me?"

"Please leave me alone! I don't want to see anything." Yelled Nancy closing her eyes and looking away.

Stefan grabbed her face and forced her to look at him.

"Please, I am married. I can't be with another man." pleaded Nancy with tears in her eyes.

"Hmm, I see. Are you sure your husband is loyal to you?" Stefan asked as he retreated.

"Not another word about my husband, you weirdo!"

"I trust him, and this is not a discussion that I want to have with a stranger in the middle of the night! I know you want to manipulate my mind."

Stefan was quiet as she kept telling him to leave. He looked like he was thinking about something.

He picked up the broken photo frame. "Yeah, I found him," claimed Stefan sounding as calm as ever.

"I can prove it to you that he is with another woman as we speak."

"Lies, you don't even know him. Plus, he is overseas in Europe selling his art." Nancy was furious. She didn't understand why he started the debate about her husband rather than raping her.

"I know he is in Wales, Ireland, staying in Hilton hotel room 242 and is in bed with one of his customers."

Nancy looked at him in shock. Did he hear their conversations? Her husband mentioned that room only once, and that was months ago before Stefan even moved into the neighborhood.

"How do you know this? Are you a spy?"

"Nancy, why would a spy be in your room at night. I am no spy." Stefan responded laughingly.

"Anyhow, dawn is approaching. I can't stay here much longer."

He converted to mist right in front of her and vanished, leaving Nancy confused. "Was that a dream?"

She couldn't sleep all night. The thought of her husbands' betrayal was too much for her to digest.

"Even if my husband is not loyal, why should I be with him? He is hot, though. Why did he leave before dawn? Could it be he is a vampire or something? Must be, that is why his gaze had magic." She kept thinking all day that day.

Nancy needed more answers. Her friends were always too drunk to give her any logical suggestion. They would have told her to fuck him anyway.

Nancy waited for nightfall and walked to Stefan's house. Samantha opened the door to allow her in. Nancy observed Samantha closely, almost comparing bust size.

"Are you his wife?" Nancy asked Samantha.

"I am one of his lovers. Stefan doesn't have wives but many girlfriends. He wants you to be one as well." Samantha replied, giving her some cookies and a cup of red wine.

Nancy was shocked at her direct replies.

"And you don't mind if he is with other girls?" Nancy further asked.

"I don't mind as long as he is happy," Sam replied.

Stefan woke up from his sleep and sensed he has a visitor. He climbed the stairs to see Nancy waiting.

He grabbed Samantha and kissed her deeply.

"Uff, don't you have any manners? Can you please wear some clothes and do your stuff later?" Yelled Nancy closing her eyes in shame.

"You are in my house, darling. My house, my rules."

"Don't call me a darling!"

"You didn't finish. How do you know where my husband is?"

"I read your mind and his too. It took a bit to connect tho. His mind was too busy in sex at the time."

"Long-distance telepathy gets challenging."

"How can I trust you?" Nancy inquired. She avoided looking at him in case she looks at the wrong body parts.

"Well, the best way is we can go to Wales," Stefan suggested.

His confidence silenced Nancy. Why would he lie to her?

"I am attracted towards you, and I think you must have figured out what I am with my stunt from last night. "

"Despite that, I won't trick you into false faith. It is not my style. I love to care for anyone associated with me. If you are not interested, I won't force you." Stefan added.

He further added, "I love it when women are passionately involved with me. Mind control has gotten boring. Feels like being with a machine."

Nancy was partly hurt that her husband might be cheating on him, and if this vampire was telling the truth, where would she go?

"You are just trying to separate me from my husband so that I can be yours,"

"I can get you without separating the two of you. It's a child play for me. I sensed sadness within your heart. All I want to do is help you move on." Stefan added in an attempt to convince her.

Nancy sat quietly for an hour drinking the wine Samantha gave her. She suddenly got up and left.

Stefan patiently waited for a few days for her to make up her mind. The decision was tough, but she was never happy with her marriage in the first place. She was a good cook and possibly could open up a bakery or something and live with Stefan. The other girls seemed to be happy with him. Maybe she would be satisfied for once too.

* * *

"I need proof my husband is cheating on me to give him divorce first," Nancy demanded of Stefan.

"Hmm, well, unfortunately, courts don't accept telepathy as proof. Let us see how to hack CCTV cameras? Do you have a laptop or something?"

Samantha was a hacker. It didn't take her long to get her husband's footage with different girls. Stefan was proud of himself for picking the right girls to feed on.

"Thank you so much. Why did you do so much for me? Wait! I remember you wanted passionate sex with me. Such a weird vampire, I would have just drunk blood and moved on if I were you." Nancy laughed.

"Aren't you satisfied with two?" Nancy further asked him.

"That is the problem. I can never be satisfied. I want more."

Stefan was amazed at how casually she said it.

* * *

Nancy finally completed the divorce process and managed to keep 90% of her husbands property. He was also to take care of her expenses for the next ten years.

It wasn't easy to get over her relationship. She was so emotionally involved even though her husband never gave her the needed attention.

Stefen took Nancy out for a date to a local bar. It was where the locals went for country music and beer. Sometimes on holidays, they would have DJ party nights.

Nancy wore a low cut mini dress with no bra allowing her boobs to hang. All evening the attention was on the duo.

The couple had a great time chatting about random things, pizza for dinner, and drank the local wine.

They left the bar relatively sober to ensure that they don't grab too much attention. Nancy was feeling a lot better with the outing.

"We can do that occasionally. I really liked it," Nancy said as they pulled into Stefan's driveway.

"So since when does a Vampire need to drive?" She asked jokingly.

Times change, I like to blend in as much as I can and be more human. The human touch helps to get girls in bed. Plus, I have way too much free time on my hands and no real goals. It is tricky to keep my mind occupied. It was hard to find a driving instructor to teach me at night, though.

They both burst into laughter. Stefan parked the car in the garage so that neighbors don't hear them.

Nancy slowly guided Stefan's hands to her breasts. She moaned as he squeezed her tits, slowly varying his pace.

She unzipped his pants, raised her dress above her waist, and sat on his dick, slowly pushing it inside. She started to rock back and forth and up and down in various combinations. She rode his dick with increasing intensity. The car squeaked as it swayed from side to side.

"It has been a while since I have had a man touch me. Thank you for letting me be the one who decides." Nancy kissed Stefan on his lips as she rocked on his dick. "ahh...bite me, I want to feel the pleasure of your fangs in me," Nancy added, offering her neck to him.

He placed both hands on the side of her face and lowered her for a deep kiss. He bared his fangs for the first time and sunk them deep into her neck. Nancy moaned as she felt the pleasure of his bite and the numbness of his sips across her body. She fell to his chest as Stefan fed on her and rocked her pussy.

Nancy moaned loudly as she was fucked her brains out. Each thrust, each touch was sending waves upon waves of pleasures through her body. Nancy climaxed earlier than she wanted and wanted more. Stefan started to fuck her again. Her chest heaving in excitement, and her body full of sweat, making her look even more attractive.

Stefan ripped the front of her dress, buried his face in between her tits. She hugged him and pulled his face deeper in her cleavage. Waves of orgasms were flooding her body. Her mind and body started to get tired as she blacked out and fell unconscious on Stefan's lap.

* * *

The next morning, Nancy woke up in one of Stefan's bedroom, feeling a bit weak. She smiled as she recalled the intense fuck from last night. She was also his girlfriend, and she loved her new life.

THE END

OTHER BOOKS BY THE AUTHOR

Karmic Love

Undercover

Eternal Love

Undying Lust

The Good Taste

Offence and Justice

A Model for Murder

Lethal Legacy

Lethal Legacy 2

Paranormal Club

Enchanted Souls

Beginners of Nowhere

Wildflower

Mystic Agent

Dark Angel

Lonesome Moonlight

The Eerie Egg

A Romantic Crime .

Passionate Alien

Dragon Knight

The Critical Case

In the Shadow

Mental Asylum

Athena

Candy Spy

Hidden Veil

Dominion

The Darkest Hour

Rachel's Journey